F

A40959

This book is due for return on or before the last date shown below.

THE GUARDIANS
OF THE HOUSE

Lucy Boston

THE GUARDIANS
OF THE HOUSE

Illustrated by
PETER BOSTON

Colt Books Ltd
Cambridge
with
Diana Boston
Hemingford Grey

Colt Books Ltd
9 Clarendon Road
Cambridge CB2 2BH
Tel: 0223 357047
Fax: 0223 65866

with

Diana Boston
The Manor
Hemingford Grey
Huntingdon PE18 9BN
in aid of
The Manor, Hemingford Grey

This edition first published 1993
ISBN 0 905899 09 1

First published by The Bodley Head Ltd, 1974.

Jacket illustration by Peter Boston

Design by Clare Byatt

British Library Cataloguing in Publication Data:
A catalogue record for this book is available
from the British Library.

Printed in England by Biddles Ltd, Guildford

1

Tom Morgan was fishing in his usual place, as far away as he could get from the noise of traffic. He came from a remote farm in Wales, but now his parents were living in a brand new factory town, all cloverleaves, tunnels, one-way streets, pedestrian bridges, and rows of tower blocks all alike. There was nothing that had grown by itself or happened by accident, and so there was neither anything familiar nor anything to surprise you.

Tom was homesick among all this newness. In the country everything is old – the fields and hills and sheep walls are old, the trees and the rocks and the footpaths, and the sea is oldest of all. In this town he felt he belonged nowhere. Where you belong is what you are.

In the centre of the town there was a large stretch of field, surrounded at regular intervals by litter bins and young trees protected by sheaths of iron railing. This was called the Park and was all that was left of what had once been quiet countryside. Through it ran, between concrete banks, a soiled river that had once sparkled through buttercup meadows and mirrored cows coming down to drink.

By the river a large corner of the Park was cut off with a dense sweetbriar hedge, enclosing a rambling garden with glades and coverts. A little side gate gave onto the river path, and this was Tom's favourite place. Over the gate he could glimpse the house far back among the trees. It was a historic leftover, a house so old that the planners had allowed it to stay. Its owner was the cause of much whispering and speculation. The children enjoyed tales of the house being haunted, and told each other they must hold a leaf of garlic in their hands when they went past, to keep away demons.

Tom was fascinated by the secretness of the house and the feeling that *there* something was really going on, different from the whirl of traffic and the blaze of shops. Often, while he was fishing from the river bank, he heard people talking about it as they went past. It seemed the house was older than it should be – was frighteningly old, but from outside the gate it only looked very much patched and mended.

"Yes, I've been inside," someone said behind his back. "You couldn't describe it. It's like something in Grimms' fairy stories. It's full of odd things, you don't know what to look at first. But I wouldn't live in it for anything.

Fancy locking yourself in alone every night with *all that*, and no neighbours near enough to hear you however you screamed."

"Yes," said another woman, "I suppose she's queer. She looks like the house, older than a person ought to be, and her clothes are as patched as the walls."

"My hairdresser said she is thought to be a witch. She talks to the birds. I've heard her. But they say she talks to mice and hedgehogs as well."

"It's not natural. It makes you wonder."

Tom thought it sounded nice. He would love to talk to harvest mice and those funny impertinent hedgehog faces. Impossible to imagine what they would say. And harvest mice would have such tiny voices. From being so often by the gate, he knew the old lady and her gardener by sight. To him, she just looked an absent-minded, ancient countrywoman in old shoes, but now he came to think about it, he guessed that if she gave orders, they would be obeyed.

It was a hot sultry day, the sort that longs for thunder to give relief. Tom had brought a mac in case of a downpour but was in shorts only. Even so he was fidgety with prickly heat, so that he couldn't settle to watch his float. There weren't many fish in this tired stream. He had a sudden longing to see inside the house for himself. He left his fishing and turned to look over the gate. The other people had moved on and were out of sight. As he watched, a car came round the curve of the far drive and stopped in front of the house. The old lady came out and was driven away, and shortly afterwards the gardener got on his bicycle and went home to dinner. At this hour there was nobody on the river bank. Now was his chance. He couldn't resist the temptation.

As his hand was on the latch of the gate, one of his schoolmates came past on a bicycle.

"What do you want in there? She'll be after you."

"She's out; I'm going to break in."

"You daren't."

"Daren't I?"

"Well, I dare you to." He cycled off, calling over his shoulder, "You'd better bring something back, or none of us will believe you."

Tom went in, circling round among the bushes and behind trees until he reached the house. Near to, it looked much more rugged and imposing. He tried peering through the lower windows, but the rooms were dark inside and all he could see was a reflection of the garden and himself with dim suggestions of the rooms behind, like two exposures on the same negative. The front door however was glass-panelled. He could see clearly inside to the strangest entrance hall. It was so full of flowers and plants and big vases of rushes and honesty, and trailing ivy and birds' nests, you would almost have to be a bird or a hedgehog to get through, and it was all doubled in large looking glasses on each side.

How was he to get in? He knew he was a trespasser, and guilty, but he was not a window-breaker. He tried the door handle. She had left it open! Was she afraid of nothing, or just forgetful?

Tom stepped in over the threshold, dropping his mac on the floor in his surprise. Inside there was an intense silence that took his breath away. All empty houses are quieter than you would think, but this silence was not just absence of sound. It was powerful, and it was decidedly not empty. He looked round among the crowded vases and leaves, both real and mirrored, for some lurking person, and became aware that many of the objects had *faces*. There were carved wooden cherubs corbelling the ends of the beams, and there were china vases with girls' faces moulded among clustering china flowers, with real flowers drooping over the china ones so that the faces just peeped out through them. All these faces looked friendly. There was an earthenware vase, mud coloured, that looked as old as if it had been dug out of King Arthur's Astolat, and this had on each side a girl's face so magically enticing and teasing that before he thought what he was doing, he had picked it up and felt it with his lips. His hand was still, with loving reluctance, putting it back on its

shelf when he noticed on the farther wall a very different face, so big he had not at first realised it was a face at all, a terrifying African mask, all straw hair and grinning teeth, with fathomless black holes for eyes, horribly eye-lashed with feathers. Out of nowhere the childish thought came into his head: that must be to chase burglars in. For real burglars, not for him. Anyway, there was no one here to put it on. And he was not a burglar, only what you might call an explorer.

Above his head someone said, "Are you a good one or a bad one?" It came from one of the wooden cherubs. Its voice was like a chisel carving out curled words. As Tom looked up, more astonished than frightened, another answered, "He doesn't know!" and laughed like wind in the shavings.

The third cherub was above the foot of the stairs. He was carved sitting on an eagle's back, and looked as uncertain as anyone would feel going up that way.

"They are waiting for you upstairs," he called down.

Tom began to climb the steep wooden stairs. What and who would be waiting up there? That too great silence was over all again. The voices had hardly broken it. One's own footsteps in an empty house are always queer, as if they belonged to someone else. Tom put his feet down carefully to make sure the sound came at exactly the time he did it, and wished

14

he made no noise. Then he trod loudly, defiantly, to out-do the house. A "hee-haw" of unbridled donkey laughter tore the silence just beside him, so that he nearly fell downstairs again. It was clarion, unbelievable, and it came from a donkey's head made in straw that hung on a closed door at the head of the stairs. It was a mask, cleverly and charmingly made, a lovable donkey with long ears, long forelock, and donkey hairs sprouting in its ears.

"So you think I'm afraid, do you, you baby-party thing!" said Tom, but he couldn't resist stroking its nose. Then, remembering the horse's head in Grimms' fairy story that gave good advice, he pushed open the door and went in.

The surprise he felt on entering was like a physical jerk, such as one feels on nearly stepping in front of a car. The castle-like hall in which he stood went right back to the Dark Ages when those old tales were first told. It was as old as a magician is old who has no age. It was as severe as the quarry from which it was taken, and as beautiful as the underside of a sheltering tree. The deep-set windows were arched as in a church, and there was a great stone fireplace almost large enough for a church porch.

In here the silence had its origin, was at its most intense and brooding. At first Tom seemed to feel it pressing into him, and then

suddenly he thought of it as an expanding emptiness, flying outwards as the stars are said to be doing. Tom strained his ears to catch any sound however slight, even the dust falling, but he heard only the singing in his own ears, and everything that had ever happened in this room, and everything that ever could happen, seemed to be there now, ready to happen again. He thought of all the people who had lived there, who had come in at one door and gone out at the other. If they could all appear at once, what a fancy-dress ghost party it would be! And yet the room, though extraordinary in itself and containing strange things, was furnished in a nearly ordinary way with chairs and tables and rugs. It was where that old lady lived. But she was out. It was empty of her. Tom remembered with a start that *they* were waiting for him upstairs. He looked round anxiously, and, of course, he now saw there were more faces up here. High above the fireplace was a piece of sculpture that might be a Malayan goddess, wearing a tall crown, very commanding. Below, on the arch of the fireplace, level with his own face, hung a small Indian head – boy, girl, man or woman, you couldn't tell – but it had a smile as soft as happy dreams, lost in delight. Across the room, on the sill of an arched window stood a boy's head, impishly mocking, beautiful and wicked. These had not at first been noticeable because they were

18

made of the same stone as the room, but once Tom had seen them, they were as insistent as if someone had said, "You can have three wishes," but frightening too. Perhaps they were some kind of test, like the three guesses or the three tasks in a fairy tale. They were all three very old. The stone was pockmarked with centuries of rain, and where a nose or an ear had been knocked off, the scar was as weatherworn as all the rest, as if to their age another two or three thousand years made no difference. They were not part of the house in the sense of being carved out of it, though the stone was similar. They must have been brought from very far away and seemed to have accepted this stonework as their own.

While Tom was looking round him lost in surprise, a ray of sunlight fell on a Chinese picture painted on a long roll of silk. It showed a prowling tiger, terribly alive, in a thicket of bamboo, and beside it in the room had been placed a large vase full of bamboo from the garden. The sun threw the shadow of the leaves over the tiger for a moment, and then disappeared as a black cloud climbed over it, darkening the room almost to night. There was a rumble of thunder, and sudden rain lashed the windows, wickedly it seemed, tearingly, like a wild beast. Above the noise a priestlike voice said, "I will show him a warning. He shall come with me. Come now."

Tom made a move in the direction of the severe goddess whose voice he thought it must be. In the lightning he saw her sitting high up, majestic and inscrutable. How could he follow? His hands, held before him in the dark, came in contact with the bamboo canes, rattling their leaves like paper. There was a blinding zig-zag of lightning and simultaneously a crack of thunder overhead, so that he thought the house must have been struck. He heard the falling of stone, and drops of rain as big as marbles struck him. He put his arms up to shield his head, and his elbows shook a shower of water off stiff leaves. Bamboo was no shelter; it only made a wetter shower bath. There was a stone archway, and under that he sheltered.

The lightning was now nearly continuous, and by its light Tom saw that he was in a steaming jungle, densely interwoven with stems and creepers and, as far as he could see, impossible to pass through without an axe. He saw that his sheltering arch was part of a large ruin, a temple or palace that the jungle had swallowed up. He wondered how long it took for such total ruin and oblivion to happen, and how it ever began. The stones of the masonry were prised apart by trees growing between them or by roots like emerging snakes. Mosses growing on the trees hung down like hair, now running with water, and loops of liana were festooned from tree to tree as if a giant vegetable spider were making webs. The scent was violent, compounded equally of growth and decay. Even the rain had a taste like coconut.

Among all this the broken temple was still impressive. Some massive weights of stone had defied all but the mosses, lichens, and ferns. The crashes of thunder left them unmoved, and the rain pouring over their surfaces made no difference in their millennia. The flickering light, the streaking rain, and the bamboo canes swaying and bending all round him, made it hard for Tom to see clearly, but presently he realised that opposite him there was a shrine built into the wall. In it a headless stone figure sat, immortal, immovable, and commanding. A gap where a stone was missing from the canopy above it explained how it came to have lost its head. A final brighter flash of lightning showed Tom, as if in a dream, a familiar head right at his feet, with the rain splashing over its closed eyelids. He knelt down to put his hands under it to feel its weight. Even the storm had lost its fearfulness and excitement for him. He wanted to put the head back on its shoulders. The temple indeed was abandoned and forgotten and in ruins, but he felt it important that there should be one majesty left to face the jungle, something you could think of and know it was there. The head weighed about as much as a big pail of water. He got it onto his knees, eased it up onto a flat

stone, and stood up to consider. The wall in which the shrine was built mounted in steps like the Pyramids, so Tom thought it not impossible to heave the stone up. The rain had stopped as suddenly as it began. The jungle no longer resounded like an army of kettle-drums, but the soft drip of leaves into pools accentuated the immense silence that now returned.

On the steps the wet moss and lichen were slippery, so that Tom knew he must be careful, going up, not to skid under the dead weight he would be carrying and crash to the bottom with it. Kneeling, he rolled it up his thighs, then with a great effort heaved it onto a step, climbed up himself, and heaved again, and again, anxious and panting. At last he reached the level of the statue's feet. Here the steps ended, and without the help of their recession it was going to test all his strength and balance to shove the head from his chest into the waiting lap. This he managed somehow, gasping and nearly bursting, then scrambled onto the statue's knees, and with his last reserve of determination got the head onto its neck. It rested steadily, the cracks fitting together. He felt a great satisfaction and sank into the lap himself to recover. A hot sky now pressed down over the treetops, which themselves became not so much shade as a smothering featherbed over the earth. Everything steamed, even the stone lap grew warm. Here and there a ray of light, finding its way through all the intercepting leaves, caught a raindrop in a blaze. Tom slept, his head on the statue's shoulder.

A movement in the jungle woke him. Someone or something was approaching – men, surely – animals would move more quietly, unless these were elephants. Lying high up in the lap of a goddess, Tom did not feel afraid. From here, he now noticed the faintest of tracks, trampled ferns and flowers and broken stems, leading from the jungle to the arch where he had found the head. Somebody had been before and was coming back. Tom drew some hanging ropes of creeper over himself and the statue. The leaf shadows played over the unchanging face so that it would hardly be seen.

Two men came along the track, the first a forest dweller, half-naked, gliding like an animal. He was there before you heard him. After him, thrusting and clumsy, came a white man. He almost fell into view, stumbling over a root and swearing. Tom distrusted him at sight. He was purple with heat and ferret-eyed. The other stood aside, contemptuous and indifferent.

"This is the place your twister of a brother brought me to," said the white man, mopping his face. "Curse it, if only one could organise a proper search – cut all this down and turn everything over, we should find as much as anyone could want. Unless, of course, your damned brother and you, or your damned father and uncles, have wormed it out already. But you wouldn't know where to sell it. Anyway, for a start, that head's going to do me a lot of good. I know a dealer who'll pay me what I like to ask. And I don't give things away either. Here we are. I put it under this arch so that I could find it again. You've got that knapsack? Where, now? You filthy scoundrel! You've taken it, you or your damn brother or your damn uncle, you slimey double-crossing clots of yellow dirt." The guide had not been listening and hardly seemed to understand. The white man seized him by the throat, saying, "I'd kill you if I could get back without you," but he broke free, shaking his head and holding up his hands in sign of innocence and protesting in his own language.

Tom stole a proud glance at the disputed head poised above him where the looters would least expect it to be. It seemed to him that its lowered eyelids flickered and that it looked at the two who quarrelled there, threatening to strangle each other in this strangling green vastness that devoured temples and hid them forever under its blind growth. And would devour these two.

Tom followed the direction of the condemning stone eyes. Behind the men, who were now standing facing each other at a loss in their rage, the leaves of a bamboo clump were moving in a way not due to the release of heavy raindrops, but to the twitching of a long tail. It was striped in black and yellow, like the pattern of bamboo leaves in sun and shadow. There were eyes too, black and yellow, nearer the ground than Tom had looked for them. There was a second's pause in which he understood that this was the avenging guardian who had been summoned; then with a whoosh like a rocket, the tiger shot out of the bamboo onto the back of the white man. He fell with hardly a gasp, cracking his head on a stone with the tiger's weight upon him. The tiger, with its glorious, shining coat and powerful dancer's movements, seized him by the neck and without apparent effort dragged the body like an empty sack, bumping over the fallen masonry and through the yielding bushes. Where the tiger alone would have passed as quietly as water through reeds, the drag of his burden was heard fading away. The guide meanwhile had escaped.

Though the statue now was still, indifferent and lost as a carved stone in the jungle must be - and more impressive for that - Tom had a feeling of being edged off. He was not in his proper place, wherever that was. He began to climb down, aware of the feeling of tooled stone under his hands. Stone was good. He brushed away some bamboo leaves that were tickling his neck, realising at the same time that his foot at the bottom had not come down as expected on leafy earth. He looked at his hand on the stone ledge, and that ledge was part of the fireplace in the old hall. Above him was the head of the jungle goddess with her all-knowing but lidded eyes, beside him the picture of the tiger.

TRITON
ROMAN · A.D. 79

2

If all this had been a dream, it was hard to shake off, and indeed Tom was much shaken. Fresh air was what he needed, so he opened a door that gave onto a balcony, and looked out. He was high up, and below him was an enclosed garden he had not seen before. It was closely surrounded and overhung by yew trees, which gave the air a greenish tinge like sea water. You could imagine it as a garden under the sea or as an enlarged rock pool. The yew tree fingers could easily be imagined as wrackweed waving under the tide, the shadowed geraniums as sea anemones opening under the fresh flow after a dry day. The wall of the house could be seen as a sheer cliff and the birds passing beneath him as fishes. Cool, after the steamy jungle.

Tom moved back into the room and, after wandering round, came to a stand by the deep-set window. In its recess stood the boy's head with its beguiling, impish, irresponsible smile. Tom now noticed that on the base was a printed label that read: TRITON, ROMAN. A.D.79. He knew what a triton was – a mermaid's son.

When the shadows of the trees moved over the window, the boy's smile came and went, and his wicked dimples too. Was it the light that was really enchanted in this room? It seemed to trigger things off. Tom grinned back at the triton. He looked much better company than that stern goddess, even if he had slept on her shoulder while tigers were about.

"You don't look much like warnings," he found himself saying aloud.

"No warnings. Temptations," said the head. "Like to come?"

"Yes," said Tom, and at once they were down in that underwater garden, swimming round among the statues and stone flowerpots and waving wrackweed, then down again in one long dive over marble stairs encrusted with sea anemones and pink and white sea fronds. The steps were disjointed and wildly tilted, as if they had slid down with the collapse of a cliff face. In places, Tom could see they were of rose pink marble. When he rolled over on his back to look upwards, the water was clear blue and what looked like the sky lay low and wrinkled, being really the surface of the water ruffled by a breeze above.

At the bottom of the stairs they came to a flat place, which perhaps had once been a forecourt, for beyond it lay the remains of a Roman villa. The ground was deep in fine white sand made of broken shells, and shells

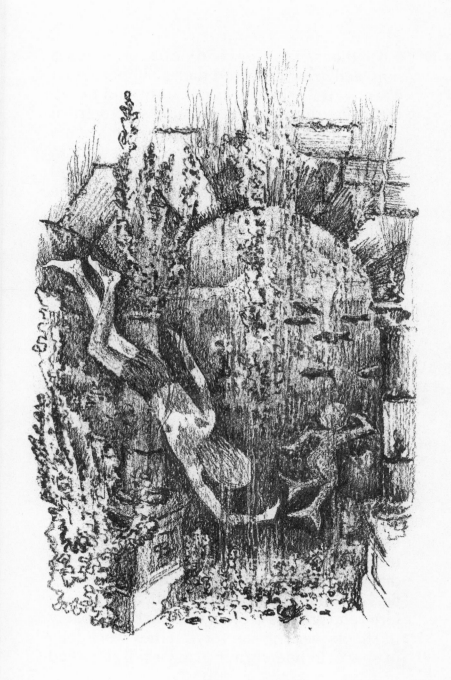

too in thousands. Trees and shrubs of glaucous seaweed grew here and there. Supported by deep water, which was constant and never withdrew, they grew in splendid symmetrical shapes, some like elms, some like palms, some like cypresses. Small coloured fish swam in and out, and Tom did too. The triton chased the fish and caught them, and let them wriggle out through his half closed fingers.

The villa, though gapped and tottering, seemed less to have slithered down on top of a landslide than to have gone down as if in a lift in some sudden land drop, such as may follow an earthquake. There were cracked arches and leaning pillars. The roof had slid away in the penetrating and lifting action of the moving sea, but as Tom followed the triton – clumsily by comparison with his fishlike speed, for he darted and zoomed round the villa – it became clear that the whole plan of the Roman house was there. They swam in through the main entrance, an important archway flanked by stone horsemen, whose seaweed cloaks floated up from their shoulders as if raised by a wind. Inside, the best rooms had once been covered with mosaic in blue and green, very suitable for the dim bottom of the sea where they had come to lie. Now, much of it had fallen off, and tiny sea ferns and grasses grew in the cracks. Probably the floors were mosaic too, but they were deep in shells. In one corner grew a tall seaweed with glossy, straplike leaves twelve feet long, such as one finds sometimes lying on the shore after a storm, but here they were upright and columnar, like an exotic tree in a grand hotel.

The triton was very much at home. This was perhaps his favourite place. He had decorated its ledges with objects found on the seabed, such as curly rainbow shells, the beautiful round skulls of drowned children who had perhaps lived here, iridescent glass phials, and an old gold watch as round and nearly as big as a tennis ball.

They swam round through doorways from one room to another. Here the owners had received, here feasted, here slept. In one room were marble benches set into the walls. Tom could sit to rest, but Triton, with his two fish tails, lay propped on one elbow in a more Roman attitude.

All the rooms opened into a central courtyard surrounded by a colonnade. Tom floated in and out of the arches and roofless rooms and was saddened by the heavy silence of the bottom of the sea. No children's voices would ever be heard here. There was not even a sound of water, for a gurgle or a splash requires air to become sound. Bubbles of speech are silent till they break on the surface. It did not strike him as queer that he needed no air. It was simply high magic.

The triton was pulling him toward the centre of the courtyard, in which grew fine

bushes of sponge rooted on fallen stone. Among them he pointed out with laughter a fountain whose basin just showed above the deposit of shells. It had been quite a large pool. In the centre was a marble dolphin with a triton on its back – this triton, Tom's triton, who seemed to think it very funny. Once it had been on the headland in the blistering Italian sun; now it was deep in Triton's own element and the unnecessary basin filled with shells. As the two of them danced round it – for anyone with a fish tail can do leaping water ballet, and Tom was also becoming fluent – their shadows wove in and out beneath them on the pearly floor. But presently their water was darkened by a shadow as big as a cloud. It hovered over the length of the courtyard. Could it be a whale between them and the sun? The triton knew what it was. He pulled Tom into hiding behind a seaweed tree.

Down from above, dangling like a parachutist, came an intruder, a diver in a full deep sea suit with his rope and his airline going up behind him to what must be a boat. Slowly he wobbled down and stood unsteadily on the shifting floor. He looked almost too awkward for action, hampered by all his gear, with heavy weights on his feet to keep him down. His movements had the eeriness of films in slow motion, and were also furtive and burglarious even in this deep sea solitude. His mask gave his face the look of a bloated fish, a horrid, unwelcome monster and up to no good. He laboured against the weight of water, playing a torch before him with which he stumbled along over fallen columns and among tough sponges. The torch picked out details here and there but made the unlit water so dim by comparison that the two watchers were well hidden.

Before long his light fell on the rim of the fountain, and then up to the dolphin, travelled over that and its gay rider, all round and back again. His slow swaying movements, like those of a drunken sleepwalker, became grotesque in an excitement unable to move any quicker. He tugged on his rope. In reply, down out of the sea-sky came loops of chain and a hawser with a large iron hook swinging like a wobbly pendulum. The diver began, infinitely slowly so that it was exasperating to watch him, to wrap the chains round the dolphin, while Triton in agitation swam round and round above him at his utmost speed, like a bat. When the chains were securely fixed and the diver put his hand out for the hook, Triton seized his air tube and squeezed it with both his small hands. The diver let the hook go, he seized his rope with frantic jerks, and his arms and legs began an uncouth dance. As the rope was rapidly pulled up, Triton let go, laughing, but the diver's weighted boot, in his frantic convulsion, had kicked the hook to one side, and now on its return swing the marble head was knocked off.

Tom let out a howl of distress, a foolish thing to do under water. His bubbles went up, up, up after the diver – and here he was, in the old lady's house, looking at that same head: TRITON, ROMAN A.D.79. He took it in his hands as if he picked it off the seabed, as if it had only that moment been broken. It was the iron that had broken its nose, but that hardly spoilt it. How he loved it! But where was that other one, his playmate? Which was the magic? If he kept this small round, smiling head, would he be able to play that game with it again, and who knows what else? He cradled and weighed it between his hands and could not bring himself to put it back. After all, the diver might have got it and kept it, though it was not his. And who could say if the old lady had any more right to it? No one, he felt, could want it as much as he did. If his mother asked him how he got it, what should he say? That he found it in the river? No, he would have to keep it stuffed away somewhere. It looked so right here in the window with the sun and leaves making ripply patterns on it. That was a pity, for he must have it.

He clutched it to him and began to make for the door, but the room had become like that other under the sea. Swarms of little fishes darted out from its shadows and surrounded him, worse than a cloud of flies. They were nibbling with bristle teeth at his face and neck and arms and the back of his knees, and

worse, they sucked. He could not brush them off while he was clutching the head. He shrugged and kicked and rubbed his legs together, but the fish were as fluid as water. In panic he remembered reading that fishes pick a man's bones as clean as vultures do, though taking a long time over it. The sensation on his flesh was revolting and his fright like a madness. He could not scream lest they get in his mouth and had to keep his eyes shut to protect his eyeballs. With his shoulders hunched to cover his ears and fishes swarming round his bare arms like sleeves, he managed somehow to lay the head back on the window ledge before he collapsed in a huddle on the floor, his head in his arms, half sobbing.

After a moment the ever-present silence pressed on his ears again, claiming his attention. Not that fishes make any noise, but probably he had, dancing a wildly as the diver on the rope. He dared to open his eyes. All was still; dust raised by his recent flapping danced in the sunlight. The triton's head lay on its side where he had put it down, smiling as if asleep and dreaming mischief.

Tom pulled himself together and stood up. This place was bewitched. Nevertheless he was ashamed, so he nerved himself to take the head in his hands again and replace it on its base. His arms looked as if he had fallen into a bed of nettles, so did his legs. What kind of a face would he take home? He took a last look

41

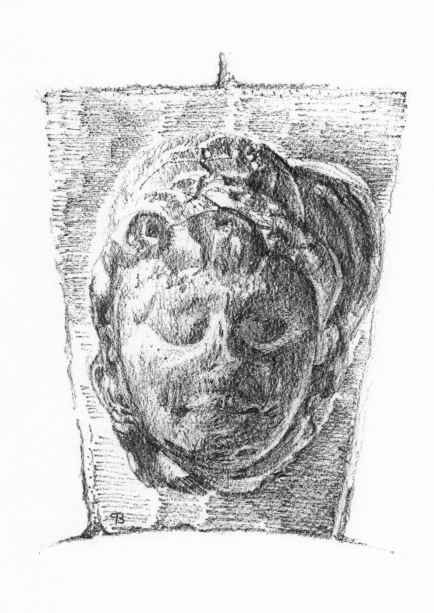

at the triton. Charming but dangerous. Not to be taken away.

Tom wandered round the room looking at all the strange oddments. They were not what you would expect to find in a witch's house – no dried crocodiles or stuffed monkeys and now he came to think of it, no cat. There was, however, a witch ball, and a beautiful glass goblet with hieroglyphics engraved on it. At night the place was lit by candles, and some of the many candlesticks were very queer indeed.

He came to a halt at last in front of the third face – the Indian with the blissful smile. There was nothing threatening or mischievous about this one, but it was altogether mysterious, and that is always captivating. Though it was stone and fully carved into a perfect face, Tom could not tell if it was man, woman, or child. The passage of time had worn and smoothed it till it was as round and soft as a rose. He stroked its surface gently.

"What is your secret?" he said.

"Those who would know must pass behind the curtain and not turn back." Had it spoken really? It looked as though it had passed beyond speech. But the curtain – what curtain? The room had many. He ran round as excited as if this was a party game. His idea of secrets was rather childish, in spite of the two experiences he had already had. Perhaps he thought of a Cloak of Invisibility, a Stone of

43

Power, or the clue to a coffin full of treasure. All the curtains seemed quite ordinary, till at last coming back to the huge empty fireplace, he saw that the back of it was not covered with soot but by a piece of black cloth on which little round pieces of looking-glass were sewn, which shone like sparks flying upwards.

Tom always acted first and thought afterwards. He pulled aside the curtain and slid in. It fell into place behind him and he was cut off.

3

He was on a dry, rocky plain under a terrible sun, a sun that did not warm but battered on his head. Behind him where the curtain had been, the land stretched to the horizon. In front of him scattered hummocks and boulders increased in number and size till they crowded together on a slope toward a distant cliff face, in which Tom thought he could discern a cave. Caves are undoubtedly the home of mystery, a prospect that quickened him. Also, once inside, if he could get there, he would be out of the fearful heat of the sun. Between him and the cliff there was not a single tree to give any shade. He set off full of eagerness, but the cave was further away than it looked. The shimmer of heat made it hard to judge distance. The cliff itself dancing before his sight might be merely mirage. Soon the sweat was running into his eyes. It was tiring to be always climbing over a rock and jumping down at the other side in order to climb the next, with the sun beating on his back and the rock hot to touch. He thought he heard voices, eerie sounds, not conversation. He wondered if sunstroke gave you hallucinations.

As he got nearer he could see that the cliff face was carved in a pattern of waterlilies with entwined stems round the entrance to the cave, but the opening was left as narrow and crooked as any natural crack in the crust of the earth. Tom reached it at last, tired and thirstier than he had ever been. As he neared the cave, he found tracks worn round the larger boulders, and when he turned the last of these, he saw the gaunt figure of a man – monk, hermit, or beggar – standing by the entrance. He was motionless but intoned in a high, resonant voice, "All is Illusion." He seemed to be addressing the vast shimmering dreamlike landscape and the sky, certainly not Tom, who reflected that those nightmare fish of Triton's were perhaps illusion. In that case this was his third illusion, but it was difficult to decide what was real when all seemed so. Dreams were sometimes more real than anything else; and wishing was the opposite of reality because you wish for what isn't, but wishing carries you along as relentlessly as a strong tidal current. It feels like a real pull. But he was too thirsty to think. His thirst was very real.

The man repeated his cry, "All is Illusion," but as he took no notice of Tom and did not question his right to be there, Tom passed by him and sidled into the cave.

47

He found himself in a long, curving hall, or perhaps he should call it a corridor. It went back and back into the hill till it was lost in darkness. The walls were high and covered all over as far as he could see, tier above tier, like a honeycomb, with carved figures seated cross-legged, all alike, and all with closed, secret faces smiling at their thoughts. So much secret smiling was overwhelming. It did not reassure him in his sudden feeling of perilous solitude. Nor did the voice of the man outside, faintly crying his ghostly message to the waste. He, Tom, was himself alone to meet the nameless fear the place held. He began cautiously to go along, looking for what else there might possibly be in the cave beside these carvings. There was generally water in caves. Perhaps he would come to some delicious trickle running into a cavity. If this was a temple, wouldn't it have holy water? Imagining the sound of water made his thirst a torment. A voice from the shadows chanted, "Thirst is Illusion." It woke echoes as if all the tiers of figures were repeating it. Tom's eyes were getting used to the darkness that had increased steadily as he went on, and he now saw a second monk squatting on the floor in the same position as all the carvings, with the same lowered eyes and indifference to Tom, though he seemed to have answered his thought.

There was here a slight curve in the contour of the cave that cut off the view of the entrance and half the remaining light, so that Tom went forward more reluctantly, crossing from side to side to make sure there were no unnoticed passages where he might get lost on the way back, already a long way. He remembered that there were often snakes in caves, and putting his hand accidentally on a cold carved leg he cried out, waking echoes like a swarm of ghosts. Though it was cold in this underworld the sweat broke out on him and he trembled. He had a horror of snakes above all things.

"Fear is Illusion," intoned another motionless squatter on the floor. The echoes broke out again, overtaking his own cry, and lessening eventually to faint whispers as they came back to him from far ahead and far behind. An echo whispering, "Fear," is spine-chilling.

It seemed to Tom now, as he forced himself on, that the echoes never ceased. What was he looking for that had once seemed so important? It was almost too dark to see anything. Strain his eyes as he might, he was unlikely to notice the chest or door or casket or roll, which he supposed would give up the secret. Perhaps it would be as small as a ring, which when he rubbed it would give him everything that he most desired. Yes, that would account for a secret smile.

"Desire is Illusion." Another lost madman, and the echoes loud over the ghost of other echoes. Illusion. Illusion.

Tom was despairing and bewildered, but a dim light showed round the next bend. Maybe it would come from another opening in the cliff. That would be a relief, for his skin crept with fear and a kind of anger. He ran towards the light, but when he got there, it was only a distant gleam of daylight relayed through a crack in the roof. It was enough for him to see that he was now in the anteroom to a special sanctuary. He had come to the end of the original cave, closed in by a slab of smooth rock, decorated like all the rest with ranks of enraptured figures, but at the base an austere but beautiful doorway had been cut right through. He could see no further. Perhaps at the other side hung the Curtain.

Tom hesitated. The echoes, reawakened at intervals by the three monks he had left so far behind, seemed to accumulate here. They made a kind of music like the trembling that follows for a long time the note of a gong. It was strangely unsettling and Tom resisted. Thirst is Illusion, he thought, but I am desperately thirsty. Fear is Illusion, but I tremble with fear. Desire is Illusion, but I desire. I desire madly to get out of here.

"You are Illusion and your name is lost." "Lost. Lost. Lost," came back from great distances.

Tom turned with tears of terror to the monk with bent head sitting there content to be nowhere and speaking desolating words.

"My name is Tom Morgan and that's who I am. And that's who I want to be."

When he heard his own angry voice re-echoing with all the other voices, it sounded to him rude and silly and not to the point, almost untrue. He shuddered.

The last echoes of "Tom Morgan" wailed away and were dismissed forever with whispers of "Illusion." From the absolute silence of the inner sanctuary there seemed to leak out the glory of something for which there was no name or word, the real secret, which filled him with fear.

"The Secret is too hard for you. But you have your wish. You are what you are."

Tom put his hands to his ears. He could not bear any more echoes, but then he opened his eyes wide in surprise. He was back where he had started, in front of the rose-soft Indian head over the fireplace, feeling sad and no good. He looked round the room helplessly. Well, he had no business here anyway. He would go out. He shrugged and put his hands in his pockets. He tried to whistle, but the note wouldn't come. He was too dry after those caves of fearful memory. He went towards the door, feeling better with every step as he left the heads behind.

4

On his way out, Tom came to the donkey's head at the top of the stairs. "That's better," he thought with great relief. "Let's have some fun." It is a release sometimes to be less than one's age. Tom put the mask over his face and looked at himself in the old lady's looking-glass. This would make them laugh at home. It was only a straw thing, not valuable. As he went downstairs he had a feeling that someone behind was pushing him, someone two steps above and stronger than he was – until he realised it was his own back legs. He looked again in the big mirror in the entrance hall. Two pretty, pearly grey donkeys standing in the hall ! That was really funny. The door was open, as he had left it, and out he capered, keen to try his new four legs. The donkey in the mirror simply slipped out and followed him, so there were two of them to kick up their heels and race round and round and in and out of the big garden. Tom had a reaction of high spirits to be let off. When he and his playmate were both blown, they halted with heaving hairy sides and amicably rubbed noses. They also agreeably nibbled each other in tickly places. They moved slowly down the garden on their neat little feet, browsing around, tasting this and that. Tom tore off some roses, very succulent and refreshing, and the thorns did not bother him, but at this point his twin started a mock fight. They turned their backs to each other and let out with their hind legs. Their hooves thudded on each other's leathery flanks, not hurting nearly so much as it sounded; then off they went for another race.

Tom had by this time worked off his sense of frustration and humiliation and was feeling a normal, cheerful animal. The grass was soft and wet, the sun warm, the sky blue overhead with black clouds scudding rapidly away. It had thundered a long time ago, he remembered, as he lay down and rolled on his back, his legs kicking wildly as they flopped first to one side and then to the other. Legs kicking wildly – that seemed to remind him of something. He brought his feet down on one side, tucked the back ones under him, and stood up. How long had he been here? What if the gardener was coming back? He began to make for the gate, not thinking that he could hardly go home like this; but his twin was upon him, heading him off and starting another mock fight. Tom tried to dodge him but felt a sharp nip on his flank. It was painful enough to make him turn with some temper, and in turning he reared and struck out with a foreleg. He received in return a real back-leg lash on the point of his shoulder. He would jolly well give that one back. The battle was ceasing to be fun. He had to defend himself in earnest, always being edged away from the gate and toward the house. Teeth came into action now purposefully, square, yellow, dangerous teeth, and kicks with hammer strength behind them. Tom fought back, but they say the animal on its own territory always wins, and at last Tom had had enough and broke away, the other still between him and the gate.

Tom with head down acknowledged himself blown and beaten. He rubbed his battered face between his knees, then on a sudden inspiration gripped it between them and pulled. The mask came off and he stood up, himself again. At the same moment his mirror twin was a boy too, wearing a mac like his, but still masked. So there are two masks, he thought. It can't matter if I take one. But who is the other boy? It can't be me because I'm this one. He picked up his straw mask and called to the boy, "Who are you? Take off your mask."

The only answer he got was a derisive hee-haw, so he strode over to him angrily and seized his straw mask by the nose and pulled. It resisted as if it was held by a vacuum, but came off suddenly so that Tom staggered back. Behind the mask there was no face. The

mac was filled with nothing, and now with flapping arms, it gave chase. Tom ran as never before, into the house which seemed the only defence, if it was one, and not the final trap. The thing came after, gaining on him, horribly close. In the entrance hall, wildly, to get rid of them, Tom threw both masks at the big mirror. They met there in a straw thud, one fell onto the floor in the mirror and one at Tom's feet. Of that dreadful thing, the only sign was Tom's own mac lying where he had dropped it when he first came in. It seemed just now to be settling into stillness.

Tom was scared beyond reason. He felt he must do something to prove to himself that he was real. His first desire was to kick that hateful mask down the hall, but as he raised his foot to kick, he thought the far more horrible African mask on the end wall loomed forward. Help ! Not that now, anything but that.

"I'll put it back!" he screamed, running upstairs to do so.

When the donkey's head was back on its hook he felt better, but came down very cautiously, looking over the banisters to make sure nothing was moving. All seemed safe. He had to pick up his mac, though unwilling to touch it and sure that he could never bring himself to put his arms through its sleeves again. He straightened the mats that donkey feet had pushed and rucked. He looked at the old vase with the girl's face he had so rashly kissed. She was the same kind of thing as Triton, elfin and up to anything, but beautiful. She still smiled and he still wanted more.

One of the wooden cherubs said again, "Are you a good one or a bad one?" and all three answered together, "He doesn't know!" and laughed like the wind in wood shavings.

Tom went out and shut the door behind him. As he walked toward the gate he tried to collect his thoughts. Everything in there was beautiful, everything was dangerous, and nothing was what it seemed, or not itself only. Perhaps the silence was the most powerful thing that made everything else happen.

He reached the gate and was gathering up his fishing things on the bank when the gardener came cycling back. All this in only an hour! His schoolmate, too, came by soon after.

"Well," he said, "did you get in?"

"Yes," said Tom unwillingly.

"Did you bring anything out?"

"Yes. This." Tom threw his mac into the river.

"What did you do that for? It's your mac."

"It's no good to me."

"What's the matter? Did they catch you there?"

"Catch me?" Tom's voice was so queer that the boy looked at him curiously.

"What, then?"

"It's unbelievable in there, and full of horrid jokes. I guess I shall have to go back there sometime to see if it's really true."

"You're boasting," said his friend, riding off. "You've never been in at all."

It's funny, said Tom to himself, with the candour that only private thoughts can have; I do desperately want to be in there again. But I don't want to be an intruder. I want to belong there.

THE END